YANKEE DOODLE IN BILLERICA MASSACHUSETS

Yankee Doodle the great hero

By

G. JORY HAN

TABLE OF CONTENTS

DEDICATED

TO

GOD ALMIGHTY

HE IS MY HEAVENLY KING, HE LOVES ME AND I KNOW.

CHAPTER 1

Great Hero

Once upon a time, in the 17th century, thirteen colonies of North America were ruled by the British government. One of the colonies in massachusetts.

There was a man who lives in billerica; a town in massachusetts, his name is Thomas Ditson. He was 33 years old farmer. A man who wish to join the minute men. The minute men are the American Revolution soldiers that wish to fight to protect their territory from colonial rule.

CHAPTER 2

Thomas Ditson in his poultry farm

He thought that he should get some fire arms and some weapons to face the challenges ahead of him. One day he left his farm and family and went to look for fire arms.

Thomas Ditson traveled to boston to see if he could get some fire arms to buy.

He inquired from the townsmen on how to go about it, and he was directed to a soldier of the British troop.

He met with the soldier whose name was Sgt John Clancy of the British troop in Boston.

He bought a great coat from him and also told him he would also loves to buy some fire arms from him.

Clancy agreed to sell him fire arms as much as he wants. Thomas also offered to take him to the country with him if he could leave the army and follow him. Clancy's anger aroused and invited some men to captured and arrest Thomas.

They locked him up so that they can punish him in next morning.

On the next morning, Thomas Ditson was brought out and was unclothed. More men gathered to tar and feathered him.

Song

"Yankee Doodle came to town,

For to buy a firelock, we will tar and feather

him,

And so, we will John Hancock"

They made him sit on a chair which was fastened to a two wheels donkey cart in a shameful manner chorusing a song to embarrass him as they pushed himthrough the streets of Boston.

"Yankee Doodle came to town,
For to buy a firelock, we will tar and feather him,
And so, we will John Hancock"

Thomas Ditson was later freed and was asked to go. He survived the incident and joined the Minute Company and later stood against the British colonial rule during the rebellion.

THE END

Full Illustration from the beginning